The Adventures of Coco

SAVING
COMET ISLAND

The Adventures of Coco

SAVING COMET ISLAND

James H. Stage

World Stage

First published in 2020 by World Stage

Copyright © James H. Stage

ISBN 9781912892884

Also available as an ebook
ISBN 9781912892686

Design by Clair Lansley
Illustration by Vince Reid
Project management by whitefox
Printed and bound by IngramSpark

To my late lovely wife Liz, a loving partner and mother.
To my late brother Ian, he was one of the good guys.
To my late father Albert, still missed by my mother
Jean and family.

Big, thank you to my son Richard, whose help and
encouragement made this book possible. I would also
like to thank my family, friends and colleagues –
you know who you are.

Contents

List of Characters

Coco – Inventor and commander of the *Flynut*

Ben – Coco's best friend

Francesca – Deputy commander of the *Flynut*

Batty and Froggy – Pilots of *Star* and *Port*

Dug – Expert digger

Grandpa Joe – Coco's grandpa

Shimmer – Grandpa Joe's old friend

Ray and Day – Shimmer's sons

Shimmer's twenty nephews and nieces

Chip the woodpecker

Chester – Leader of the council

Mr Tramp the sea turtle – Grandpa Joe's old friend

Digger – Dug's dad

Hamish the golden eagle

Nessie – Monster of Loch Ness

Lucky the rabbit

The owl

The tarantulas

THE CROWS

Crook – Leader of the gang

Hooper – Crook's second in command

Tom, Chick and Maggie – Gang members

THE HUMANS

Corey and Freya – Schoolchildren in Aberdeen, Scotland

Daddy and Mummy – Corey and Freya's parents

Mr Stagg and Mrs Mair – Corey and Freya's teachers

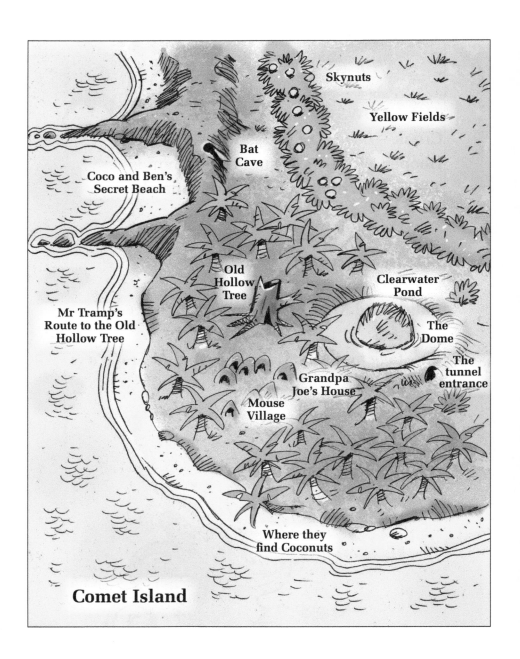

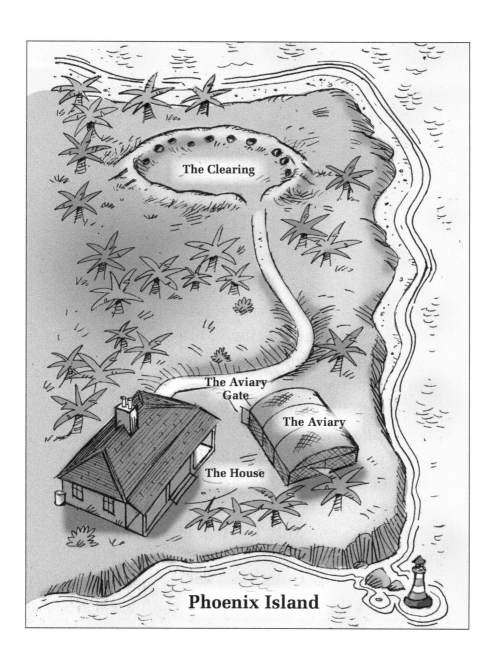

The Clearing

The Aviary
Gate

The Aviary

The House

Phoenix Island

Chapter 1

Coco's Life Changes

Coco kicked at the warm sand with his little feet. He was heading slowly towards his best – and only – friend Ben, who was waiting for him on their secret beach.

'Where have you been?' asked Ben, his nose twitching impatiently.

'Oh, just watching the skynuts. I wanted to see which ones got highest in the sky before the sun started to dip,' replied Coco.

'So which one did? The big, fat one like me or the shy, thin, small one like you?' asked Ben.

'You're not fat. It's only when you stand next to me that you look bigger,' replied Coco. 'But the shy, thin, small one went the highest!'

'I don't think so,' said Ben, as he playfully pushed his friend into a small incoming wave. 'I watched them too, while I was waiting for you.'

'Okay, Ben, they were both equal,' laughed Coco as he shook the seawater from his fur.

Just then, out of the corner of his eye, Coco spotted one of the descending skynuts behaving strangely.

'Ben, look over to your left. Can you see that firefly on the skynut?'

'Yes,' said Ben. 'We've seen that before!'

'But can you see something odd happening?' Coco persisted.

'No,' said Ben.

'The skynut's stopped falling, and the firefly isn't flapping its wings!' said Coco.

'And?' said Ben.

'That has to mean the firefly is mimicking the sun and using its light to make the skynut rise again!'

'How fascinating. Not,' said Ben, rolling his eyes. 'We should be going home, before your skynuts start bombarding us!'

Ben stood up, and as Coco got up too, he heard a strange noise. 'Can you hear that whooshing sound!?' he asked Ben.

The sound was rapidly getting louder. What was making it?

As they turned around to see, they were met with the terrifying sight of an owl swooping, legs outstretched towards them! Before they could scurry away, it grabbed them in its massive, sharp talons, and swiftly lifted them up into the sky.

Coco, who was squeezed tight in the owl's left claws, screamed across to Ben in its right claws, 'Try not to struggle! The fall would kill us!'

Hardly able to breathe, Ben replied, 'We've got to do something or as soon as we land, we'll be eaten!'

They stared at each other in terror as they were carried higher into the darkening sky.

Just as they were beginning to give up hope, they were suddenly bombarded with descending skynuts. A large one hit the owl directly between its huge eyes, causing it to slacken its grip on the two mice.

'Look, I'm free!' Coco called to Ben. He had managed to crawl onto the owl's leg. Then, by chance, some slowly descending skynuts had come alongside him. Terrified, Coco had seized his opportunity and leapt across the gap. Now, holding on tightly to the skynut, he shouted, 'Come on, Ben, wriggle your way free. We can use the skynuts as parachutes!'

'I can't!' Ben replied. 'The owl's got me with both claws and its talons are digging into me!'

As the light started to fade, the owl was battered by fast-falling skynuts. The bird was now forced far out to sea, away from Comet Island.

'Don't give up!' Coco shouted after Ben. 'I'll try to find you!'

Ben replied tearfully, 'Goodbye, my friend.'

Coco sobbed as he watched his friend disappear from sight. Then he felt himself starting to slip from the skynut. Looking down, he saw two more nuts falling slowly, side by side. He lost his grip and fell, but managed to grab them – one with his front paws and the other with his feet.

Below, he saw the beach rushing towards him. Coco closed his eyes . . . and crashed into the soft sand with a mighty thump.

Coco lay there unconscious as darkness descended and the tide came in, lapping at his paws.

* * *

Grandpa Joe was waiting nervously for his grandson Coco to return home.

Grandpa turned to Shimmer, his best friend and the largest flightless firefly on the island. 'I'm getting really worried,' he said. 'It's way past Coco's bedtime!'

'Let's go and look for him,' Shimmer replied. 'We'll go along the stretch of beach where we last saw him. I'll light the way.'

'Okay,' said Grandpa, and they headed off into the night.

The sand was cold beneath their feet as they searched. After some time, Shimmer turned to Grandpa.

'We're running out of beach,' she said, as she peered into the gloom.

'Turn up your brightness, as high as you can,' Grandpa told her. 'We really have run out of sand. There are only these huge rocks. I'll search between them.'

As Shimmer waited in the same spot for several minutes, helping Grandpa to see, she noticed something odd hovering in the darkness beside her. 'Joe,' she said, 'there's a skynut floating in the air next to me.'

'Yes, very strange,' agreed Grandpa as he peered into the distance beyond the skynut. 'Hey, there's a small beach hidden on the other side of these rocks!'

'I'm getting too old for this kind of thing,' Shimmer replied as she climbed up to see. Then, looking along the little beach, she said, 'There's nothing here. Just a bunch of skynuts at the shoreline.'

Grandpa looked in their direction. 'No, I can see something else.'

They moved closer. 'That's Coco amongst them!' shouted Grandpa as he ran towards the shore. He reached Coco just as a wave was about to engulf him, and he lifted him away from the water. 'He's still breathing,' said Grandpa. 'Let's get him home as quickly as possible.'

'I'll light the way,' Shimmer replied. 'Can you carry him?'

'Yes,' replied Grandpa. 'He hardly weighs a thing.'

*   *   *

The next morning, just as Coco was beginning to stir, Ben's mother arrived at Grandpa's house. 'Have you seen my son?' she asked him.

'No. Was he with Coco?'

'I think he was. When he went out, he didn't say where he was going.'

Ben's mother crossed over to Coco's bedside and asked him quietly, 'Was my Ben with you last night?'

'I . . . I . . . can't remember,' mumbled Coco, before falling back into unconsciousness.

*　　*　　*

Several days later, as Grandpa and Ben's mum nursed Coco, a small mouse ran in.

'Who are you?' asked Grandpa.

The mouse was too out of breath to speak.

'She's Francesca, from Coco and Ben's survival class,' replied Ben's mum.

Thanks to all the commotion, Coco woke up and started to listen to what Francesca was trying to say.

'I know where Ben is!' she spluttered in-between deep breaths.

'Where?' Ben's mum demanded, before Coco could speak.

'Two weeks ago, Chip the woodpecker vanished. Now he's back, and he's got some news.' Francesca paused for a breath. 'He's just telling our leader, Chester. He'll be here shortly.'

Coco sat up in bed. 'I remember now,' he said. 'Ben and I were caught by a huge owl. I escaped but Ben was carried out to sea.'

'Oh no!' shrieked Ben's mum.

Just at that moment, Chip landed outside the open door, wafting dried leaves into the air.

'Gather round,' he said excitedly. 'I have some good news and some bad news.'

'Tell me the good news,' Ben's mum said tearfully.

'Well, the good news is . . . I think Ben is still alive.'

Ben's mum and Coco both jumped into the air with joy. Grandpa grabbed and hugged Coco, and told him to take it easy.

'Chip, calm down and tell us how you came by this information,' said Grandpa.

'Remember that terrible night I went missing?' said Chip.

'Yes, but how does that relate to Ben?' asked Coco, overcoming his shyness.

'Well, that night, I was flying home to roost when suddenly a tornado sucked me high into the sky – so high that I had ice on my beak! The next thing I knew, the wind dumped me somewhere I'd never been before. I found out later it's called Phoenix Island.'

'Please tell me what happened to Ben!' pleaded his mum.

'I am! The next day I found loads of food in a clearing. But suddenly a net was thrown over me . . . I was captured by some humans and put in a massive cage with hundreds of crows!'

Chip pecked at Grandpa's doorframe to clear his head before continuing.

'About four days ago the humans caught a huge owl and released it into our cage. The owl told us how he'd been captured in a net, and the big, fat mouse he was about to eat had managed to escape down a rabbit hole.'

Ben's mum wept tears of joy as she turned to Coco and said, 'You've got to find Ben, Coco. He's your best friend.'

'I will . . . ' replied Coco. 'I WILL!'

Then Grandpa turned to Chip and asked him sagely, 'What's the bad news?'

'The crows,' replied Chip. 'They organised the escape from the cage, and now they're headed here. The owl told them Comet Island is full of big, fat mice!'

Chapter 2

Crow Invasion

The next day, Coco was lying in bed trying to figure out a plan to rescue Ben when someone started banging at his door.

'Who is it?' Grandpa called out.

'It's me, Francesca. Open the door, quickly!'

As soon as Grandpa started to open the door, Francesca squeezed impatiently through the gap.

Coco pulled the blanket over his head so that he could pretend to be asleep, and listened.

'They're here!' said Francesca. 'The sky is black with them.'

'You mean the crows?' demanded Grandpa.

'Yes, crows! Hundreds and hundreds of crows!

Chester wants us all to come to an emergency meeting inside the Old Hollow Tree.'

Francesca went to leave, but then paused and asked, 'Where's Coco?'

'He's in bed, hiding under the blanket,' replied Grandpa.

'Why? Is he scared of the crows?' asked Francesca.

'Probably,' said Grandpa, 'but also shy of you! Tell Chester we'll be there as soon as possible.'

*   *   *

Coco cowered behind Grandpa as they made their way to the Old Hollow Tree. There was a strange noise in the distance.

'What's that terrible screeching sound?' asked Coco.

'I think it must be the crows feeding on the skynut bushes over at Yellow Fields,' replied Grandpa.

'I think we should hurry up!' said Coco, anxiously.

'Yes, I think we should,' replied Grandpa, picking up the pace.

As they approached the Old Hollow Tree, Coco saw a giant turtle sticking his head into the entrance. 'Who's that?' he asked.

'That's Mr Tramp,' replied Grandpa, squeezing past the giant turtle to get inside.

'Hello, Grandpa Joe,' said Mr Tramp as Coco and Grandpa came to a halt alongside his face.

'Grandpa, move forwards!' urged Coco.

'I can't, Coco', replied Grandpa. 'It's crowded in here.'

At one end of the space inside the tree, standing on a rock, stood Chester, leader of the mice and all of the other animals.

'Listen up,' he said, addressing his audience. 'I know everyone's scared of what's happening on our island. The crows have started eating our favourite food, and when they run out of skynuts, according to Chip we'll be next on the menu.'

'Yes, that's right,' said Chip. 'An owl told Crook, the crow leader, that Comet Island

was full of big, fat mice. Crook's scary – you can recognise her by her crooked beak. Then there's her second in command, Hooper – you'll know him as he has a hoop on his leg . . .'

The crowd was beginning to get noisy and anxious, when suddenly Mr Tramp boomed, 'I know who can get rid of the crows.'

'Explain,' urged Chester, as the crowd fell silent.

'When I was a young turtle, my curiosity drove me to explore all of the Earth's oceans. Our ocean has a warm Gulf Stream that flows northwards, towards a distant country called Scotland, which is surrounded by a cold sea. While swimming close to Scotland's coast, I could taste fresh water, so I followed it up the river to a massive lake, called Loch Ness, which was deeper than the sea. I dived down to explore a hidden cave . . . and, suddenly, a huge, dark monster came straight for me out of the gloom with its mouth wide open! At the last moment it spotted my flippers and, for some reason, it turned away.

'I swam to the surface as fast as I could and there the monster scooped me up on to its nose. As my flippers dangled in the air either side of its head, I could feel a vibration coming from between the monster's eyes. To my surprise, it began to speak to me. "Hello, fellow flipper creature," it said. "I was about to eat you, but your flippers caught my eye. Lucky for you."

'Why was I lucky?' I asked nervously.

'"Because your flippers look similar to mine," replied the monster.'

'Get on with it, Mr Tramp,' shouted Chester impatiently.

'Okay. After our frightening encounter, the monster and I became great friends and spoke of many things, including a golden bird that terrifies everything that flies.'

'So we've got to find this golden bird to rid us of the crows?' asked Chester.

'That is correct,' said Mr Tramp. 'But it would take me too long to swim all the way to Scotland, and no ordinary bird would have the strength or the courage to approach the golden bird, let alone to search for a monster to ask for directions to find it!'

All the creatures in the hollow tree were filled with a mixture of fear and hope.

'I think I have an idea,' whispered Coco to his grandpa. 'An idea that will get us to Scotland, using skynuts!'

Before Coco could whisper any more, Mr Tramp announced to the crowd, 'There is a very small mouse, next to my ear, hiding behind his grandpa. He has an idea involving skynuts, to get us to Scotland!'

The crowd groaned with disappointment. They all knew Coco was the shyest, smallest, most timid mouse on the island. Nobody believed he would have anything useful to say.

Grandpa, Mr Tramp and an embarrassed Coco were pushed to one side as the crowd forced their way out of the tree – heading back to their homes before dark. Chester was soon the only other creature left inside.

Coco, still hiding behind his grandpa, said, 'Let's go home. No one wants to hear my idea.'

'Just a minute, Coco,' said Chester. 'I want

to hear your idea.'

'You tell him, Grandpa,' said a shy Coco.

'I don't know what your idea is, Coco. You tell him,' said Grandpa.

'Come on, Coco, don't be shy,' Chester encouraged him. 'Comet Island needs something to hope for.'

You can do it, Coco thought to himself. *Think of Ben.*

'Okay,' said Coco. 'I . . . I . . . have an idea, to build a flying machine, using skynuts and fireflies . . . all inside of a clamshell . . . and . . . and other things I haven't thought about yet.'

'Interesting idea,' said Chester. 'Come and demonstrate it to me and the rest of the island council as soon as you can. We are desperate!'

Chapter 3

The First Flight

As Grandpa and Coco walked home from the meeting, they could hear the shrill squawks of the crows in the distance.

'I'm scared,' said Coco.

'So am I,' replied Grandpa. 'But you've got to focus on your idea.'

'I am . . . I will,' said Coco. 'Could you help me with building and experimenting?'

'Of course,' said Grandpa. 'We'll start as soon as we get home.'

'Good,' said Coco. 'Could you also ask Shimmer to come along to help us? We need something to show Chester and the council tomorrow.'

*   *   *

Looking out of the window, watching the sunset, Coco said to Grandpa, 'We have to go to Yellow Fields to find a ripe skynut for the experiment.'

'Okay,' said Grandpa quietly, opening the door.

Francesca was right outside, along with her friends Batty and Froggy. She had been just about to knock.

'Where are you going?' she asked.

'To Yellow Fields, to find a skynut,' replied Grandpa.

'Can we come and help you look?' asked Francesca, hopefully.

'Only if you're quiet. I suppose the more eyes we have to search, the quicker we'll find one ... But why are you all here, anyway?'

Francesca explained as they made their way to Yellow Fields. 'We heard Mr Tramp say at the meeting that Coco had an idea to get to Scotland, to find the golden bird. It would be so exciting for us to help you.'

Soon they arrived at Yellow Fields, where nearby some crows were perched feeding on the yellow, knobbly skynuts. 'Keep quiet and start looking for a ripe-rise skynut,' whispered Coco.

'What does a ripe-rise skynut look like?' asked Francesca, quietly.

'They have an orange tinge.'

'There . . . over there, hanging from that bush!' Francesca pointed with her little paw. 'Is that what you're after?'

'Yes,' said Coco. 'Grandpa, Batty, Froggy, keep a lookout for crows. Francesca and I will go and get the skynut.'

Then they crossed the clearing to the bushes and Francesca started to pull at the nut.

'Come on, Coco, help me,' she said.

But just as Coco was reaching up to help, the skynut snapped free from the branch, causing the bush to whip back with a loud rustle.

A nearby crow heard the noise and flew over to investigate.

'What have we here?' he said in mock surprise. 'Two scrawny mice!'

Coco and Francesca froze in fear as they saw he had a hoop around one of his legs. Hooper's massive black beak started to open as he moved in towards them . . .

Suddenly, in the distance, there was a loud, urgent squawk!

Hooper winked at the petrified mice, grabbed the skynut that they had found, and gulped it down. 'It's your lucky day – that was Crook calling. The two of you together wouldn't make much of a snack, anyway . . . Must fly,' said Hooper, and off he went.

'I'm so sorry,' said Grandpa. 'That crow appeared from nowhere!'

'Never mind,' replied Coco, although he was shaking with fear. 'Are you okay, Francesca?'

'Yes,' she replied. 'Just a bit stunned.'

'Froggy, Batty, there's a skynut hanging above you. Grab it quickly and we'll get it to Grandpa's workshop before the crows come back,' commanded Coco.

He was surprised at his own daring, and everyone else looked at him in amazement. But they did as he said.

*   *   *

When they arrived at Grandpa's workshop, Shimmer was waiting for them, along with her twenty nieces and nephews. They had brought a large clamshell that Grandpa had asked them to collect from the beach.

'Come on, let's all get inside before the crows spot us,' said Grandpa.

When everyone was inside, Coco shyly began to ask, 'Please all . . . all . . .' But he was too embarrassed to say any more.

'I think Coco is trying to say we should lift the clamshell onto the table,' said Francesca.

Coco nodded in agreement.

Grandpa realised that Coco needed some encouragement. 'Coco, look how you took command down in Yellow Fields! You can do it. Time is of the essence.'

Coco replied slowly, not just to Grandpa, but to everyone. He took a deep breath. 'I . . . I . . . am shy. I have got to change, I want to change. Grandpa and Ben believe in me. I must start believing in myself.'

Everyone smiled at Coco as they all lifted the clamshell onto the table. And Coco smiled back, unembarrassed.

'Please, Froggy and Batty, can you lift and glue the skynut to the bottom half of the clamshell? Then, Shimmer, can you sit on top of the skynut?' said Coco, more confident by the minute.

'This is hard work,' said Shimmer, as she struggled to find a comfy position on top of the skynut.

'So far so good,' said Coco. 'Next, everyone help lower the top half of the clamshell.'

'Hold on a minute,' said Shimmer. 'I'll be in the dark!'

'Not for long,' said Coco as he motioned to the team to continue.

'What next?' asked Shimmer, becoming a bit anxious once the top half was in place.

'Gradually increase your firefly light,' Coco told her.

Everyone stood back as a strange orange glow glimmered through the narrow gap between the two halves of the closed shell, getting brighter and brighter.

Francesca squeaked in amazement as the shell began to slowly lift off the table.

'What's happening?' shouted Shimmer anxiously.

Coco shouted back, 'You're flying above the table!'

'I haven't flown for a long time,' replied Shimmer in a muffled voice, as she shifted position on the skynut.

The shell began to swing from side to side. 'Don't move!' Coco shouted to Shimmer.

Everyone dived out of the way as the shell bounced off the walls.

'Shimmer, stop glowing!' shouted Coco.

Shimmer started to dim, but it was too late! She crashed through Grandpa's door and came to rest among some bushes. Everyone rushed outside to help her.

Coco knocked on the side of the shell. 'Are you all right, Shimmer?'

Slowly the shell opened.

'That was tremendous, Coco! It was fantastic to be able to fly again,' she said.

'It was fun and frightening watching you, but what happened to make you flightless?' asked Coco, awkwardly.

'Remember last year, when the Comet flew over Comet Island and some of its fragments landed in Yellow Fields?' asked Shimmer.

'I do,' acknowledged Batty.

'Well, I flew over to investigate and got too close to one of the brightly glowing embers, and that's when my wings were scorched!' Coco looked sad, but Shimmer continued enthusiastically. 'But after the accident I realised my light had increased massively.'

'Thank you for telling us about it,' Coco said. 'But before we all go home, let's head down to the beach to discuss what just happened.'

'Can we not leave it until tomorrow?' pleaded Batty. 'We're all tired.'

'No,' replied Coco, 'as Grandpa said, time is of the essence.'

*   *   *

Everyone followed Coco down to the beach, where they sat beneath the largest coconut tree.

'Okay, Shimmer, tell me what movements you made while flying the clamshell,' said Coco.

'When I slipped forwards on the skynut, I seemed to be flying forwards. And as I moved to the right it felt as if I was flying to the right.'

'Well, that matches what I saw,' replied Coco, his interest overwhelming his shyness.

Shimmer looked worried. 'You don't expect me to fly to Scotland on my own, do you? There's no room for anyone else!'

'I know,' said Coco. 'That flight was just a test. What we need is a huge shell, big enough for a crew and provisions.'

'That was the largest clamshell we could find,' explained Grandpa.

'We could build a flying raft,' suggested Francesca.

'It's an idea,' said Coco, 'but we'd be vulnerable to crows.'

As they all scratched their heads, trying to think of an idea, they noticed Mr Tramp had emerged from the sea and was making his way towards them.

'Hello, Mr Tramp,' said Coco, as the turtle slid down the slope next to them. He accidently hit the base of the tree, bringing a massive coconut crashing down into the sand in front of them.

Brushing the sand from his fur Coco exclaimed, 'That's it. That's it!'

'That's what?' asked Francesca.

'Can't you see?' asked Coco as he jumped on top of the coconut. 'This is our shell!'

'But it's not a seashell,' said Grandpa.

'It doesn't have to be a seashell, as long as it protects the crew from crows. Thank you, thank you Mr Tramp,' continued Coco.

'You're welcome,' replied the turtle, proudly.

Chapter 4
High Noon

The next morning, Coco awoke with the sun streaming in through his window. As he looked outside, he noticed with dread that more crows had arrived, away in the distance, at Yellow Fields.

'Wake up, Grandpa,' said Coco anxiously. 'We have a lot to do today.'

'Okay,' said Grandpa, with a yawn. 'You'd better wake Froggy, Batty and Shimmer. And don't forget Digger and Dug. They arrived late last night.'

'Who are Digger and Dug? And where are

they?' enquired Coco.

'They're moles – you know Dug, he's in your survival class. Digger's his father. And they're probably still sleeping in their mound, next to my gumtree.'

Coco went outside. As he approached the mound, he started to feel shyness coming over him. 'I mustn't let this stop me from finding Ben,' he told himself.

As he got closer, he saw his classmate Dug, half inside and half outside the mound.

'Hello, Dug. Why are you here, and why are you halfway out of the mound? The crows will see you.'

'Hi,' said Dug. 'You know, this is the first time you've actually spoken to me.'

Coco realised that his shyness had been stopping him from being friendly. *I've got to change my behaviour if I want to find Ben,* he thought. 'Sorry,' he replied, trying to be confident.

'It's okay,' replied Dug. 'Well, the first reason I'm halfway out of the mound is that I'm scared of the dark, and the second is because your flying idea is amazing! I really want to help,' replied Dug. As Dug followed Coco to the clamshell, Coco realised that making new friends felt good.

'Come on, everyone,' instructed Grandpa. 'Batty, Froggy, Shimmer, Digger, and Dug, lift the clamshell . . . Okay, fireflies go in below the shell and take some of the weight . . . All right your side, Coco?'

'Yes,' replied Coco.

'Okay your side, Francesca?'

'Yes, okay this side. Everyone has their share of the load,' replied Francesca.

'Then let's head towards the Old Hollow Tree. We have a meeting with Chester and his fellow councillors,' Grandpa instructed.

They were struggling with the heavy clamshell, still a long way from the tree, when Coco realised there was a better way to get his invention to Chester. 'Stop, everyone!' he said. 'Lower the shell. Why are we struggling? Let's use brain over brawn!'

'What does that mean?' asked Francesca, with a puzzled expression.

'Shimmer, please climb inside the clam shell,' Coco asked her, 'and slowly start to glow.'

Everyone stood back and watched in amazement as the clamshell lifted gently into the air.

'This is freedom and why I wanted to be part of the team!' said a delighted Dug.

'Francesca, give me a hand attaching this line to the clamshell to help us steer it,' said Coco.

*   *   *

As they approached the entrance to the Old Hollow Tree, Chester and the council were there to meet them, standing and gazing in awe.

'Come on in,' Chester motioned to Coco and his friends. 'This is fantastic! Can you make it land?'

'Yes,' said Coco nonchalantly. 'Shimmer, can you slowly stop glowing?'

'Okay, Coco, I'll stop.'

Then to everyone's shock, the clamshell crashed to the ground, knocking up clouds of dust!

'I said SLOWLY stop!' cried Coco, forgetting

himself in dismay.

'Sorry about that, Coco. All I heard you say was *stop glowing,*' said an embarrassed Shimmer.

'That's okay,' said an equally embarrassed Coco.

'Right,' said Chester. 'That was a bit unfortunate, but I get the principle. Can you explain to me and the council what your plans are for the mission to Scotland to find the golden bird?'

'I . . . I . . . ' stuttered Coco, still trying to overcome his embarrassment.

'Let me explain,' said Francesca, confidently taking control of the situation. 'We've found a super-large coconut . . . '

'It's okay, Francesca,' said Coco, as he regained his composure. 'Let me explain my idea. The clamshell floats in the air because the skynut is glued to the shell, and when Shimmer starts shining her light on the ripe skynut – mimicking the sun – the skynut rises, lifting the shell with it. But the clamshell is only the prototype – the first attempt at a design. For the journey to Scotland we would need to build a bigger vessel using the largest coconut on Comet Island and two smaller ones attached to it on either side. Once the coconut water and most of the white coconut is removed from inside of the three coconut shells, there will be enough room for the crew, spare skynuts, honeycombs and the remaining coconut for food.'

Chester turned round and addressed the council. 'What do you think of Coco's idea?'

The council conferred, and then told Chester that they thought it could work – but only with the right commander and crew.

Francesca shouted excitedly, 'Choose me to lead the mission!'

'Well, you're certainly confident enough,' said Chester.

'Hold on,' said Coco. 'I might not be as confident as Francesca, but I know how everything works!'

Chester thought carefully, then said, 'We, the council, have decided to call the flying machine, the *Flynut*. Coco, you will be in charge of building it, and Francesca will help you. When it is built and we're ready for launch, the council will choose the commander and crew. Until then, we'll be watching you both.'

'We need a secret place to build the *Flynut*,' piped up Grandpa. 'My workshop isn't big enough, or safe enough to protect us from the crows.'

Chester looked around and asked, 'Has anyone got an idea where we could build the *Flynut*?'

There was silence, until Froggy suggested, 'Why don't we move to the tall reeds in Clearwater Pond?'

Then Batty spoke up. 'Yes, I've seen it from the air and there's a large mound of earth in the middle, covered with reeds.'

Everyone looked at each other in dismay, realising that most of them would have to swim to reach the mound in the middle of the pond.

Then Francesca asked Dug, 'Do you think it would be possible to tunnel underneath the pond and hollow out the inside of the mound from below?'

'Yes,' said Dug. 'There is one problem, though,' he told the team, looking ashamed. 'I'm scared of the dark!'

Chapter 5

The Great Dig

Chester turned to Coco and Francesca. 'All of Comet Island's resources are at your disposal. That includes its inhabitants – frogs, fireflies, moles, mice, bats and birds.'

Francesca nodded. 'Coco, as you have the expertise, you take total control of the *Flynut* construction and I'll take charge of the dig,' she said confidently.

Chester smiled at Francesca, impressed with her and realising that after the *Flynut* departed, the dome would be the safest place on the island. 'Let's make it happen!'

I've got to up my game, Coco thought. *Francesca wants to be chosen for commander of the mission. But it should be me!* He turned to Francesca and said, 'You've got to dig the tunnel quickly. I can't build the *Flynut* until you've finished!'

'Well, help me then,' said Francesca.

'All right,' said Coco. 'I have an idea to help Dug overcome his fear of the dark. Shimmer, could you ask your nephews Ray and Day to buddy up with Dug and light his work area?'

'That's brilliant! I mean, really brilliant,' said Dug gratefully.

Coco positioned himself at the entrance to the tunnel and helped to scatter all the soil being carried out by Francesca's team.

After they'd worked for a couple of hours, Coco looked at the amount of earth scattered around him.

'We must be getting close to the centre of the mound,' he said.

'Yes,' said Francesca, 'I'll go back down and give the order to start excavating the dome.'

Chester and the councillors, who were working and watching the operation at the same time, were impressed with her.

*   *   *

Later on that day, Coco went down the tunnel to see what progress Francesca had made.

'This is amazing,' said Coco. 'But remember to stop digging when you come across the roots of the reeds!'

'I'm not stupid,' Francesca retorted. 'Fireflies, please light up the dome.'

Everyone stopped work and gazed up in total amazement.

'I can hardly believe it,' said Coco. 'It looks like the night sky, but brighter!'

'Now it's over to you to start building the *Flynut*!' Francesca told him.

'Okay,' said Coco, 'but there is one more thing you have to do.'

'What's that?' replied Francesca, with a puzzled look.

'Once we've built the *Flynut* it will have to launch through the roof of the dome,' said Coco.

'I hadn't thought about that,' replied Francesca.

'Well, I have,' said Coco. 'What you have to do is ask Chip to cut a plughole in the roof of the dome, big enough to allow the *Flynut* to pass through with plenty of room to spare.'

'But when Chip cuts the plughole, the plug will fall down into the dome,' said Francesca.

'Not if he cuts the hole at a slight angle so that the top is wider than the bottom,' Coco explained. 'That way the plug won't fall into the dome. Then the birds, bats and fireflies can lift it to allow the *Flynut* to pass through and then lower it back into place afterwards.'

'Hold on a minute,' said Francesca. 'If our team will be able to lift the plug, I'm sure the crows would too!'

'I never thought of that,' replied Coco, crestfallen.

'Well, I have,' said Francesca, getting back at Coco for his previous smugness. 'But it's easy to stop them. The plug has reeds growing on it, and so does the area around the plughole. Once the plug is back in, we just tie the roots of all the reeds together.'

Chapter 6

Building the Flynut

'Coco, how wide is the *Flynut* going to be, so I can tell Chip what size to cut the hole in Dug's dome?' asked Francesca.

'How come we're calling it Dug's dome now?' asked Coco.

'I suggested it to my friend Chester,' replied Francesca.

I've got to become more confident, Coco thought. 'Francesca,' he said, 'come down to the beach. My team and I will show you the three coconuts we've selected.'

As they approached the coconuts where they lay halfway up the beach, Francesca asked Coco, 'Why do we need three of them?

One looks big enough to me.'

'Well, I've calculated that the flight to Scotland will require a very large coconut to hold everything we need to complete the mission. Unfortunately, as you know, this is the biggest one we could find.' He indicated the biggest coconut. 'That's why we need the additional space in the two smaller coconuts, which will be attached to the large one.'

'I understand,' said Francesca. 'Coco, hold on to this end of the string so that I can measure the coconuts.' After they were finished, she went on. 'Okay, that's it. I must get back to Dug's dome and give Chip the measurements.'

'Good luck, Francesca,' said Coco as she set off. Then he turned to the others. 'Right, team, we have to roll these coconuts back to the dome.'

Dug looked at Coco with his eyes wide.

'Sorry, I meant Dug's dome,' said Coco reluctantly.

'It's okay, Coco, just call it the dome. Francesca was playing with you,' said Dug.

They hadn't gone far when Batty started to

protest. 'How much further do we have to go? I could fly to the dome and bring back some helpers.'

'No,' said Coco. 'The crows will spot you. Just keep pushing, quickly now. We're almost there.' But just then he spotted shapes in the distance and exclaimed, 'I can see some crows flying towards us!'

'Coco, these coconuts are really heavy to roll,' said Froggy.

'I know,' Coco replied. 'Everyone keep moving. I'll run ahead and get help!'

As Coco arrived at the tunnel entrance he could see the crows getting even closer. He shouted inside, 'Francesca, quickly. Help us get the coconuts into the tunnel. The crows are almost here!'

Francesca called to those in her team who were working near the entrance. 'Hurry, if the crows see these coconuts it'll give away our plan!'

Francesca and Coco's teams joined forces to hurriedly push the coconuts to the tunnel. But as they gathered speed, the animals couldn't keep hold of them and had to let the coconuts go. They went careering down the slope towards the dome!

Francesca shouted to the far end of the slope, 'Fireflies, flash your lights to warn everyone to clear out of the way!'

Luckily those still down there were able to press themselves against the sides of the dome as the coconuts thundered past. They crashed into the stores that were neatly stacked up waiting for the mission and rolled to a stop.

'Move fast,' said Coco to Francesca. 'Everyone, help pull the tunnel door shut . . . '

'Just in time,' said Francesca. Through a small gap in the door they could see Crook and Hooper landing close by.

'Everyone keep quiet,' whispered Coco.

'They're poking the door with their beaks!' whispered Francesca fearfully.

'It should be okay,' said Coco. 'The door is made of thick branches and reeds that blend in with the rest of the undergrowth!'

Outside, Hooper turned to Crook. 'I'm sure I saw movement here somewhere.'

'Let's search over this side,' said Crook, seeming impatient.

'They're moving away from the door,' whispered Coco, 'but they're still searching nearby. Francesca, could you keep an eye on the crows? I have to go and start building the *Flynut*.'

'Yes,' said Francesca. 'But don't make any noise. I'll let you know when it's safe.'

Coco silently scampered down to the dome and told everyone to be as quiet as possible.

'Okay, team, listen up,' he said. 'Chip, when we get the all-clear from Francesca I want you to peck hatches and windows in the three coconuts. The rest of you, give me a hand to tidy up all these stores ready for the mission.'

'All clear!' they heard Francesca shout down the tunnel, and all the fireflies turned on their lights.

'Right, Chip, get pecking on the lines I've drawn on the coconuts,' said Coco. 'Remember to cut the holes at a slight angle so that the windows and hatches can be secured if we come under attack.'

'What do you mean, *if*? It's *when* we come under attack!' said Francesca as she joined in the clear-up.

*   *   *

'That's the rear access hatch finished,' said Chip. The large coconut had been cut and drained and the first hatch had been pecked out.

'Okay, Chip, keep chipping,' said Coco. 'Ray and Day, come with me inside the coconut and turn on your lights.'

In they went. 'This is amazing,' said Ray as he lit up the bright white interior.

Batty and Froggy climbed in behind them. 'So this is going to be our flying machine?' said Froggy.

'No,' said Coco. '*Your* flying machines will be attached to either side of this coconut with magnets. Before we can do that, you need to chip off all the white coconut, except for half of the ceiling.'

'Okay,' said Froggy, 'but why leave any

white coconut on the ceiling?'

'That's going to be our food for the mission!' replied Coco.

'But what about us? We can't eat coconut,' said Ray and Day together.

'I've thought of that,' replied Coco. 'There will also be honeycombs stuck to the other half of the ceiling.'

'Whoopee!' yelled Ray and Day as Francesca joined them.

'The honeycombs are for us, not you, Francesca,' they warned her. 'We love honey!'

'So do I,' replied Francesca indignantly. 'Coco, can you tell us how the *Flynut* will be assembled? And most importantly, how do we fly it?'

Reluctantly, Coco agreed to tell her. He was giving away his advantage when it came to being chosen as mission commander, but she would need to know.

'Ah, Shimmer, I'm glad you're here,' Coco began, as his friend arrived. 'You need to know what I'm about to say as well. But first we should name the three coconuts. Any ideas?'

'Yes,' said Froggy. 'I'm naming my ship *Port* as it's positioned on the left-hand side.'

'And I shall call mine *Star*,' said Batty, 'because it will be on the right.'

'Okay,' said Coco. 'That leaves the large middle coconut.'

'I know,' said Francesca, 'as *Port* and *Star* are smaller, how about *Mother*?'

'I was thinking *Ben*,' said Coco, shyly, thinking of his friend. This whole mission was for him.

'It would be confusing to have two Bens,' Francesca objected.

'All right, if *Mother* makes you happy, then so be it,' replied Coco reluctantly. He turned the conversation back to the construction of the *Flynut*. 'Batty and his friends from the bat cave have been collecting pieces of magnetic ore. When Chip finishes pecking all the holes, we'll put them in place.'

'What will that achieve?' asked Francesca.

'We'll use the magnets to close the windows and hatches. Every magnet has a north end and a south end. If you put north and south ends together they'll join up. So, if you attach the north pole magnets around the hatch and window frames and the south pole magnets around the hatches and window covers, when they're closed they'll seal the *Flynut* against attack,' said Coco.

'If you say so,' replied Francesca with a quizzical smile. 'That leaves the last question: how do we fly it?'

Everyone looked at Coco with expectant expressions. It made him feel very self-conscious!

'Well . . . well . . . ' he stuttered.

'Come on,' said Batty. 'I know how to fly, but this contraption is weird!'

'Weird it may be,' replied Coco, twitching nervously, 'but it's our only chance of saving Comet Island and finding my friend Ben. Okay. So this is how I think it will work. The *Port* coconut with Froggy and Day in it will have a skynut glued to its floor, as will Batty and Ray's *Star* coconut. That leaves us with Francesca and Shimmer – not to mention Shimmer's twenty nephews and nieces and twenty spare skynuts – in *Mother*.'

'Not so fast,' said Francesca. 'Why do we need Shimmer's twenty nephews and nieces? And why do we need spare skynuts?'

'We'll be depending on Shimmer's nephews and nieces for backup light during our long journey. We need the backup skynuts, which will need to be protected from light as they only have a limited anti-gravity lifespan.'

'I understand,' said Batty. 'And how do we control the *Flynut*?'

'We just have to learn as we go along,' replied Coco. 'Everyone must do their best.'

'Yes,' said Francesca, 'but can we practise first?'

'No,' said Coco. 'Time is running out!'

Everyone looked at each other. They realised a huge challenge lay in front of them.

Froggy turned to Francesca and said, 'I don't think I have the courage to learn to fly *and* get up close with the monster and the golden bird!'

'We're all scared,' Francesca replied. 'But what's the alternative? To be eaten by crows!'

Chapter 7

The Launch

Grandpa and Chester made their way down the tunnel towards the dome.

'Well, Chester, have you selected the commander of the *Flynut* yet?' asked Grandpa.

'I'll tell you when we get th—,' Chester started, then he and Grandpa stopped in their tracks and stared up in awe at the *Flynut*. 'That's amazing,' he breathed.

'Glad to see you both,' said Francesca confidently as she squeezed her way past Coco, Froggy and Batty.

'We at the council have decided that the commander of the *Flynut* and the mission will

be . . . Francesca! said Chester.'

'Congratulations, Francesca,' said Coco, as he made his way slowly towards the rear of the *Flynut*.

'Hold on a minute.' Francesca turned to speak to Chester and Grandpa. 'I am very flattered,' she warned Chester, 'but I will have to decline the job in favour of Coco!'

'Why?' asked Chester with a puzzled look.

'Coco is a team player. He told me things about the *Flynut* and crew arrangements that are important for the success of the mission, which I in turn explained to you, as if they were my own ideas. If it was the other way around, I would probably have kept them to myself.'

'It's very selfless of you to give the position to Coco,' said Chester.

'Thank you, Francesca!' said Coco, giving her a big hug.

'Okay, now that's settled,' said Chester, 'Coco, you will be commander and pilot. Francesca, you will be deputy commander and co-pilot. Shimmer, you are in charge of Ray and Day and all twenty of your nephews and nieces. Froggy, you are pilot of the *Port* nut, with firefly Day. Batty, you are pilot of the *Star* nut, with firefly Ray. Dug, I am afraid we've run out of room in the *Flynut*, but thank you for all your enthusiasm and input.' Chester paused, then added, 'One last thing! Coco, you can't be shy if you want to fly. To succeed, you must try!'

'Thank you, Chester, I will do my best,' said Coco. 'Okay, everyone to their positions inside the *Flynut*.' He turned. 'Hey, Dug, I'm sorry there wasn't any room left for you.'

'I'm sorry too,' replied Dug, sadly.

'When we get back, I'll need your skills to search for Ben in the rabbit holes on Phoenix Island.'

'Good luck, Coco,' said Dug – just as Coco tripped over one of the ropes that was tethering the *Flynut* to the ground.

'Okay, is everyone in position?' asked Coco as he climbed aboard the *Flynut*, hoping no one had noticed him stumble.

'Yes.' Francesca was laughing at Coco's mishap.

'That's enough,' said an embarrassed Coco. 'Let's get started.'

'I just about forgot,' said Grandpa as he handed over a mysterious little package. 'You will need this to find your way to Scotland.'

'What is it?' asked Coco.

'No time to explain,' replied Grandpa. 'Here's a letter, along with instructions. Now hurry, there's a storm brewing. The team are all in position and starting to lift the plug.'

Coco looked up through the front window of *Mother* and saw soil starting to fall from the plug as it was slowly lifted by the outside team.

'Right, Shimmer, light up gradually,' said Coco.

'Ray and Day, follow my lead,' said Shimmer, through the hatches into *Star* and *Port*.

All three skynuts began to emit an *mmmmmmmmmmmmmmmmmmm* sound as Shimmer, Ray and Day pressed their bright yellow light against them. Francesca, sitting alongside Coco, looked around inside the *Flynut* and marvelled at what was happening.

Everyone turned and looked at one another in astonishment as the *Flynut* hovered centimetres above the ground.

'Hold that light level, Shimmer,' shouted Coco.

'Coco, the tethers are beginning to strain!' Francesca said.

'Cut them all at the same time,' shouted Coco to the ground crew.

One of the ground crew was a bit too hasty and cut the port tether ahead of the others. This made the *Flynut* tilt sharply. Everybody fell sideways and the craft spun wildly.

'Stop all light output,' shouted Coco to Shimmer.

The *Flynut* shuddered to a halt as it hit the ground.

'What's happening?' came a shout from the top of the dome. It was the team leader of the twenty bats and twenty fireflies who were struggling to lift the plug.

'It's okay,' replied Coco. 'Get ready to raise the plug higher as soon as we lift off. Francesca, help me get Shimmer back onto her skynut!'

'Coco, do you know what you're doing?' asked Shimmer, as they struggled to get her back into position.

'Yes,' said Coco. 'Now start your light output again, slowly.'

'That's it, we're flying again,' said Francesca.

'Steady as you go, Shimmer . . . Okay, hold that light output level. We're right up against the base of the plug,' said Coco.

Coco then shouted through the vent-hole of the plug to the lifting team, 'Okay, raise it!'

'It's too heavy!' replied the team leader.

'Okay, listen up,' said Coco. 'Keep your team lifting the plug, and we'll help with pushing it as hard as we can. Right, Shimmer, give me full light output.'

'Okay,' said Shimmer, as the inside of the *Flynut* glowed brightly from the yellow of the fireflies and the orange of the skynuts, which made a deafening sound . . . but the *Flynut* took the strain.

'That's it, we're lifting! Make it quick, we can't hold for much longer!' shouted the plug team leader.

'Shimmer, move to your left, fast,' ordered Coco.

'We're free,' shouted Francesca as the *Flynut* slid and scraped away from underneath the dome plug.

Coco looked over Francesca's shoulder. 'Yes, we're free. And the plug team have managed to lower it perfectly back into position.'

Froggy shouted excitedly across to Batty, 'Now we are free!'

Chapter 8

Flight into the Unknown

Down on the ground, a pair of crows noticed an orangey-yellow light in the distance.

Hooper turned to Crook. 'Is that a skynut?'

'No,' said Crook, the crow leader, 'skynuts don't go up at night, they come down. Wake Tom, Chick and Maggie. We'll fly up to investigate.'

*   *   *

Inside the *Flynut*, Coco was unwrapping the package Grandpa had given him.

'What is it?' enquired Francesca.

'I don't quite know,' said Coco. 'It has a large metal needle that's pointed at both ends, balanced inside a wooden box with the letters N.E.S.W. marked inside it.' He held it up and it shot through the air, sticking fast to one of the magnets that secured *Star*'s shell to *Mother*'s.

'I think we should read the letter Grandpa put in with it,' said Coco.

The first sentence of the letter read, 'KEEP THE COMPASS AWAY FROM MAGNETS.'

It continued, 'Its needle will always point north. It is to be used at night or when flying through cloud. GOOD LUCK! GRANDPA. '

'I'll fasten the compass by the three front holes in *Mother*,' said Coco to Francesca.

Just at that moment, a big black beak jabbed through the top window!

Francesca shrieked. 'Shimmer, increase your brightness!'

But Shimmer couldn't hear anything above the squawks of the attacking crows. The *Flynut* was now out of control!

'Maximum brightness, Shimmer!' screamed Coco, as he managed to crawl alongside the firefly.

'You've got it, Coco,' Shimmer replied. 'Max light!'

The *Flynut* immediately shot upwards, leaving the crows far below.

Coco commanded, 'Francesca, Froggy and Batty, secure all windows and hatches. Shimmer, change your position to full speed ahead.'

Ray and Day copied Shimmer's actions as the *Flynut* thrust forwards, causing everyone inside to fall backwards.

'Now,' said Coco as he regained his balance, 'we will use the compass to find our way to the land of the golden birds.'

Unknown to the *Flynut* crew, one of the rear access hatches had not been closed properly, and light was spilling out into the night sky. Far behind, Crook and her gang could just see it.

* * *

'Francesca, we've been flying for quite a long time now,' said Coco, as he looked at the compass needle pointing northwards. 'Tell the crew to have a meal break. I reckon we'll be in Scotland by dawn.'

An increasingly strong westerly wind was pushing against them and they struggled to keep the *Flynut* heading north. The sky began to darken and heavy rain started to fall, battering them towards the east coast of Scotland.

'Open the front observation windows on all three ships and look for an emergency landing area!' instructed Coco.

'I can see an area just to our left, beyond those two houses,' shouted a rain-soaked Froggy.

'Okay, Shimmer, move to your left . . . Brace

yourselves, everyone, it looks like we're going to hit the roof of that house!' said a frightened Coco. 'Shimmer, maximum brightness!'

But the *Flynut* did not respond fast enough. It glanced off the roof of the house then continued down into the garden . . . and smashed through the window of a treehouse!

Inside the house, two children, Corey and Freya, were woken by the noise. They looked outside to see what had hit their bedroom roof.

Corey turned to Freya and said, 'Can you see that dim yellow light in our treehouse?'

'Yes,' replied Freya. 'But it's too dark and stormy to go outside. We'll have to wait till morning to see what it is.'

When they eventually fell back to sleep, Corey dreamt that the light was a meteorite and Freya dreamt it was a fairy. Little did they know it would turn out to be something far stranger!

* * *

The next morning, before their mummy and daddy got up, Freya and Corey ran down the stairs and excitedly pulled open the back door.

'Me first, Freya,' said Corey.

'No, me,' said Freya.

As they slowly approached the treehouse, they could hear small, squeaky voices coming from inside. Peering in through the broken window, they saw lots of tiny hovering fireflies that were lighting up three coconuts, two mice, a frog, a bat and a larger firefly with their glow. All the creatures looked dazed and bewildered.

'Hello,' said Freya.

On hearing her voice, the creatures panicked and dashed behind a toy treasure chest in the corner of the treehouse.

'It's okay,' said Corey, 'there's no need to be frightened.'

Coco peered out from behind the chest and said, 'Well, don't talk so loud!'

'Can you talk a little louder?' Corey replied.

'YES,' shouted Coco, speaking a lot louder

now. 'My name is Coco and this is my co-pilot Francesca. We've been blown off course and need help to rebuild our ship. Can you help us? We have to be on our way today and time is running out to save our island.'

'Yes, of course we will,' whispered Corey, amazed at the talking mouse. 'My name is Corey, and this is my sister Freya.'

'Well,' shouted Francesca, 'we are running short of food – honey and coconut – and need directions to find the monster and the golden bird.'

Just as Corey was about to reply, the children's mother shouted from the back door. 'Come back inside and have your breakfast or you'll be late for school. Now!'

Corey whispered, 'You mice had better come with us and give us more information.'

Coco looked at Francesca, then said warily, 'Yes, but before we go . . . ' He turned to Froggy, Batty and Shimmer before continuing, 'please do as much as you can before we get back.'

'Okay, that's it,' said Corey. 'Coco, jump on my hand and I'll hide you in my hoodie.'

'You too, Francesca,' said Freya. And she popped the little mouse into her hood, to avoid detection.

As they sat down at the breakfast table, their daddy asked, 'What have you two been doing outside?'

'Oh,' said Freya, 'we were looking to see what caused that bang on the roof last night.'

Just at that moment, Francesca moved through Freya's hair, not realising that her whiskers were tickling the girl's ear. This made Freya giggle loudly.

'What's so funny?' asked Daddy.

Before Freya could answer, Corey interrupted. 'Yes, we climbed up to the treehouse to see if we could see anything.'

'So did I. I got the ladder out earlier and had a quick look at the roof,' said Daddy. 'It's not damaged. I'll have a proper look around when I get back from work.'

'Mummy, do you have any honey, and a coconut?' asked Corey.

'No,' said Mummy, 'but I'll buy some from the shop on my way home from work . . . It's good to hear you want to eat healthily! Okay, off you go to school, and mind the traffic!'

*   *   *

As they made their way to school, Coco shouted in Corey's ear, 'Tell Freya to come closer so we can talk.'

Freya leaned her head towards Corey's.

'That's perfect,' shouted Coco. 'We need you to tell us where we can find the monster . . . '

'And the golden bird that lives in Scotland,' interrupted Francesca.

Corey looked at Freya and asked her, 'Do you know where these creatures are?'

'No, but we could ask our teachers,' replied Freya, as they arrived at the school gates.

'Okay,' said Coco. 'Francesca, if and when you find out where these creatures are, come and find me, and we'll go back to the treehouse and help ready the *Flynut* . . . Time is running out to rescue everyone on Comet Island.'

'There's just one problem,' said Corey.

'Some people are scared of mice!'

'What are you two whispering about?' asked Freya's teacher, Mrs Mair, as they approached their separate classrooms.

'Nothing,' replied Freya.

'Well, Corey, hurry along to your classroom. Mr Stagg is about to start his short talk on climate change,' Mrs Mair instructed.

*   *   *

Later that morning, Francesca crept out of Freya's hood and whispered into her ear, not realising she was tickling her, 'Hurry up and ask the questions!'

'Excuse me, Mrs Mair,' said Freya as she burst out laughing. 'Do you know where in Scotland the monster lives?'

'Stop laughing,' said Mrs Mair, trying to keep a straight face. 'It's not funny. Legend has it that there's a monster in Loch Ness. Her name is Nessie.'

'I'm sorry, Mrs Mair. Thank you for that information. What does "loch" mean?'

'It's a Scottish word. It means lake.'

'One more question, Mrs Mair. Where do the golden birds live?'

'I have no idea, Freya. Now carry on with your work.'

Meanwhile, Corey was putting the same questions to his teacher, Mr Stagg.

Mr Stagg replied, 'I don't know anything about a monster, but I think your golden birds are probably golden eagles. They can be found on the Isle of Skye, off the west coast of Scotland.'

Coco crept out of Corey's hood and shouted in his ear, 'Thanks, Corey! I'll go and get Francesca and head back to the treehouse to help repair the *Flynut*.'

Suddenly, the girl sitting next to Corey saw Coco and screamed. The whole class erupted as Coco ran, zigzagging his way out of Corey's classroom and across the corridor into Freya's classroom. Chaos broke out there, too, as Francesca climbed down from Freya and ran towards Coco.

'Quickly, follow me,' said Coco, as they

dodged the huge shoes of the enormous children who were escaping to the playground.

Back inside the school, the headmaster was in a state of panic, standing on a chair and called for Mrs Mair. 'What are we going to do, Mrs Mair?'

'Get down from that chair for a start,' she replied. 'It looks like the whole school is infested with mice! We must declare an emergency and send all the children home!'

*   *   *

Coco and Francesca were scurrying along as fast as they could.

'What's that creature up ahead?' asked Francesca as they made their way along the pavement. 'It's looking at us!'

'I don't know, but it's showing its teeth!' said Coco, thinking this was the end. 'It's about to pounce!'

Suddenly, Freya and Corey came running up behind them.

'Now, calm down, little pussy,' said Freya,

grabbing the cat's collar.

'That was close,' said Corey as he quickly scooped up Coco and Francesca.

'Thank you, both,' said Coco. 'What kind of monster is that?'

'It's a cat,' said Corey, as he put Coco back into his hood. 'Put it down, Freya,' he said and when the cat had scarpered away he placed Francesca into her hood.

'When we get back,' shouted Coco to Corey, 'put us straight back in the treehouse. We have a lot to do. Just one more thing, can you explain to us what Mr Stagg was talking to the class about – climate change and low-lying islands being affected by rising sea levels?'

'It's only if the polar ice caps melt a lot,' replied, Corey with a worried look.

As Corey and Freya approached their house, they noticed their mother's car in the driveway. 'Quick,' said Coco, 'take us to the *Flynut* and find out if your mother has the food. And can you draw us a map of how to get to the monster?'

'Okay, Coco. We'll be back as soon as we

can,' said Corey.

'Hello, Mummy,' said Freya. 'You're back early.'

'Yes, I am,' said Mummy. 'I got a call from your school telling me something about mice.'

'Did you get the honey and coconut we asked for?'

'Yes, but you're not having a snack until you've done your homework.'

The children went upstairs to their bedroom.

'Leave the homework,' Corey said, as he flicked through the pages of his atlas, looking for Scotland.

'Stop!' exclaimed Freya. 'And turn back two pages. There it is.'

'Find me a piece of paper and a pencil,' said Corey.

Corey began to draw a map of Scotland. When he was finished, he highlighted Loch Ness and the Isle of Skye.

'There,' he said.

'Okay, move over, Corey, and let me colour it in. They need to know the difference between land and sea,' said Freya.

'Good job,' said Corey when she had finished. 'Let's go downstairs and get the honey and coconut.'

Freya and Corey raced downstairs and headed for the back door.

'Where are you two going?' asked Mummy.

'To our treehouse . . . Can we take the honey and coconut with us?' asked Corey.

'Why do you want to take them outside?' said Mummy with a quizzical look.

'We don't want to eat them yet, we want to draw them! We've never had a real coconut before,' pleaded Freya.

'Okay, but don't be long. Your daddy will be home soon and we'll have supper. And don't leave any food in the treehouse . . . We don't want to attract any mice, do we?'

'Of course not!' said Corey, smiling at Freya.

As they approached the treehouse, Freya said to Corey, 'We have to cover the broken window before Daddy comes back to check the roof of the house.'

'Yes,' said Corey. 'And I have the very thing, my pirate flag!'

Freya quietly opened the treehouse door and whispered, 'Hello. We've brought the coconut, honey and map.'

'Good,' said Coco. 'Can you lift me, Francesca, Shimmer, Froggy, Batty and the ships up to the small table?'

'Yes,' said Freya, as she knelt down to pick everything up.

'There,' said Corey, as he finished putting the pirate flag over the window. 'It's quite dark in here now, though.'

'No problem,' shouted Coco as he turned to Shimmer and her crew of fireflies. 'Turn on your lights.'

Suddenly the whole table was bathed in yellow light.

'This is magical,' said Corey. Then he opened up the map. 'Okay,' he said to Coco, Francesca and the crew, 'this is where we are.' He pointed to a city marked on the map. 'You can see that Aberdeen is on the east coast of Scotland, and if you follow my finger as I move it to the left you can see Loch Ness. This is where Nessie the monster lives. And

further left we come to an island off the west coast of Scotland, called Skye. This is where the golden eagles live.'

At the mention of the monster and the birds, Batty and Froggy began to shake with fear.

'Why do you want to find these creatures if they scare you so much?' asked Corey.

'We need the help of Nessie and the golden birds to save our island from marauding crows,' replied Coco.

'I see,' said Corey. 'So, now you know where you're going, how can we help with the repairs to the *Flynut*?'

'Well,' said Coco, 'the ship is held together by magnets. Please can you join the two smaller coconuts to the mother coconut?'

Freya held the mother coconut as Corey took the smaller ones in each hand. As he moved them closer the north and south magnets attracted and the small coconuts suddenly flew from his grasp and stuck rigidly to each side of *Mother*.

'Well done,' said Coco. 'Would you now open the honey jar for us?'

'Okay,' said Freya as she lifted the jar of honey and the new coconut up onto the table. The fireflies formed a line between the jar and the entrance hatch to the mother coconut. Freya scooped the honey from the jar and put it into a tiny toy cup from her play set. The honey was then passed along the line into the ship, where Shimmer filled the hexagonal cells inside the empty honeycombs.

Shimmer called out from inside the ship, 'Stop, we're full up.'

Coco looked at the coconut that Corey and Freya had supplied. 'How are we going to get inside to get the white stuff out?' he wondered aloud.

'How did you manage to get the white coconut out when you built the ship?' Corey asked.

'Chip the woodpecker helped us,' Coco replied.

'Hm,' said Corey. 'I don't know any woodpeckers.'

'I have an idea,' said Freya. 'We could climb up Daddy's ladder and drop the coconut onto the path to break it.'

'Brilliant!' said Corey, and they made their way towards the house.

When they got to the ladder, Freya climbed to the top, but just as she was about to drop the coconut, Daddy came out of the house and shouted at her to come down immediately! Freya dropped the coconut, which smashed into small pieces.

Daddy was very angry, shouting, 'That coconut could have been your head!'

He climbed up the ladder and carried her back down to the bottom. 'Corey, you clear this mess up and then come back into the house. You are both grounded!'

Corey quickly gathered up as many of the small pieces of coconut as he could carry and ran back to the treehouse with them. The crew, who had been watching what had been going on, thanked Corey for all his and Freya's help. Coco told Corey that they were going to take off as soon they loaded the white coconut, and head towards Loch Ness.

Just as Corey picked up the honey jar,

Mummy shouted to him to come back into the house immediately.

'I probably won't see you again' said Coco. 'Thank you both for helping us.' Then he started to organise the launch. 'Batty, fly up to the window and remove the pirate flag,' he said. 'The rest of us will separate the white coconut from the shell and load it into the *Flynut.*'

Batty did as he was told, but after a while he came back down again. Out of breath, he said to Coco, 'I couldn't manage to get the flag off. It's still attached.'

'We'll just have to fly through it,' said Coco.

'There's one other thing,' continued Batty. 'The crows have followed us and are eating the coconut on the path!'

'Okay,' said Coco, 'let's get inside the *Flynut.*' Once they were inside he turned to face the crew. 'We have two problems,' he said. 'The first is that we need to fly through the pirate flag without getting snagged in it. The second is that we need to fly as fast as we can to avoid the crows – they've followed us and they're waiting outside.' Batty and Froggy looked at each other with fear in their eyes.

Coco ordered Shimmer to start lighting up. Ever so slowly, the *Flynut* started to rise.

'Okay, Shimmer, move forwards on your skynut,' said Coco.

Ray and Day did the same, following Shimmer's lead.

'Give me full power,' said Coco.

The *Flynut* shot forwards, snagging the pirate flag and ripping it off the window frame.

'I can't see where we're going!' said Coco. He reached through the window and ripped a hole in the flag that was now draped right over the *Flynut*.

'Okay, I can see now,' said Coco. 'Shimmer, move slightly forwards and keep giving full light.'

The *Flynut* shot up at an angle, narrowly missing Corey and Freya's bedroom, where the children were waving goodbye through their window. As Froggy opened the rear entrance hatch of *Port*, he spotted the crows following

at a distance. They seemed to be frightened of the flapping pirate flag.

Coco looked at the compass, and directed them west. 'The next stop is Loch Ness to find the monster!' he told the crew.

Batty and Froggy glanced at each other worriedly, then turned and looked into the distance.

Chapter 9

Monster Hunt

As the *Flynut* flew westwards through the night sky towards Loch Ness, Francesca asked Coco, 'How are we going to find Nessie the monster in that vast loch?'

Coco replied, 'I think Nessie will find us.'

'How will she do that?'

'Well, at night we'll fly low and slow and criss-cross over the loch, with the fireflies forming a V-shape either side of us. Hopefully Nessie will think we're a golden eagle.'

As dawn broke, the crew were all looking out of the windows, trying to spot Loch Ness in the distance.

'There, there!' shouted Froggy, pointing to a

gap in the mist. 'I can see the loch.'

'Okay, turn to the right,' Coco instructed Shimmer.

The loch appeared to get bigger as they approached it. Francesca spotted an old derelict castle on the shore. Coco instructed Shimmer to dim slowly so they could descend to the castle and land.

As they glided through an opening in the castle wall they could hear a strange wailing sound coming from beneath the floor.

'Shimmer, shut down,' called Coco. As the *Flynut* landed, he called to the crew, 'Batty, I want you to find out what that wailing sound is and then fly over the loch to see if you can find any signs of Nessie. Froggy, I want you to swim around the loch looking for her.'

*   *   *

Later, Batty returned. 'Any sign of Nessie?' asked Coco.

'No,' said Batty, 'but I did find a small sandy beach with some huge tracks on it.

They looked like the marks Mr Tramp makes.'

'Sounds promising,' said Coco. 'What about that wailing sound?'

'Oh, that was a group of children, blowing into bags and moving their fingers over pipes with holes in them, for some reason. There are no stairs up to here, so they can't get to us.'

'Thanks for that, Batty,' said Coco. 'We're still waiting for Froggy to get back from her mission, but we'll keep an eye out for her as we search for Nessie. Francesca, can you cover for Froggy in *Port* and remove the pirate flag? We don't want to frighten Nessie. Okay, Shimmer, slowly light up.'

Slowly the *Flynut* lifted into the darkening sky.

'Okay, stand by,' said Coco. 'Fireflies, get into a V-formation outside and keep close to the *Flynut*. We want Nessie to think we're her old friend the golden eagle.'

The *Flynut* skimmed across the surface of the water in a criss-cross pattern.

Suddenly Batty exclaimed, 'There, up ahead! It's the beach where I saw the flipper marks.'

Then, out of nowhere, a huge wave appeared, heading straight towards them.

'Quickly,' said Coco. 'Close all windows and hatches.'

The fireflies broke formation and flew high into the air to dodge the wave. The *Flynut* was plunged into a swirling torrent of water. When it eventually bobbed up to the surface, Coco ordered the front windows to be opened.

The fireflies hovering overhead lit up the scene. The crew gasped in fear as they saw a pair of giant jaws gaping wide, exposing huge teeth and lunging towards them . . . And inside was Froggy – alive!

Froggy jumped out of Nessie's giant mouth and hopped up on top of her head.

Seeing Froggy helped Coco overcome his fear. He instructed the *Flynut* to hover above the monster's nose. Froggy moved to sit between her eyes and started to explain what had happened.

'I was swimming in the middle of the loch, searching for Nessie, and I got a bit tired. So when I spotted a floating tree trunk, I climbed

on top of it and fell asleep.

'Later on, the log began to rise out of the water! I saw a pair of enormous eyes open and then cross, looking at me between them. When I got over my shock, I explained to Nessie – yes, that is her name – our mission and why we are here. To avoid being detected, Nessie doesn't roar or speak, so the only way to communicate with her is to position yourself between her eyes and pick up her vibrations.'

Coco told the crew to land the *Flynut* on Nessie's nose. As they landed, Batty ran to the back of the ship, terrified.

Coco climbed out of the *Flynut* and slowly approached the spot between Nessie's eyes. His whiskers started to twitch as he began to sense the vibrations.

Nessie began to communicate using ultrasound vibrations. She was asking how her old friend Mr Tramp was doing.

'He's in good health,' replied Coco. Pressing his paws firmly against Nessie's skin, he added, 'Do you know where we can find the golden eagles on Skye?'

'Yes, I do, but before I tell you, promise me that in the event of monster hunters coming you will help divert them away from my beach. My eggs are buried there.'

'Most certainly,' assured Coco.

'I only know one golden eagle, and he is the biggest. His name is Hamish,' replied Nessie.

'Whereabouts on Skye does he live?' asked Coco.

'You must keep flying west. When you arrive at the Isle of Skye, turn north at the Fairy Pools, then shortly after that you will come across the Old Man of Storr, which is a massive natural rock tower. That's where Hamish lives!'

Just at that moment there was a flash of white light and the roar of a ship's engine. It was the monster hunters! Nessie quickly dived into the deep.

This left Coco and Froggy splashing about in

the water. Francesca took control of the *Flynut* and shouted out of the window, telling them to climb on top of the craft. Once they were on top of the *Flynut*, Coco shouted to her, 'Don't go back to the castle yet. I promised Nessie I would lead the hunters away from this area . . . Head further down the loch.'

The *Flynut* quickly rose up and then zoomed away, with the hunters following in hot pursuit.

As Coco and Froggy hung on for dear life, Coco shouted to the fireflies, 'Listen up. I'm going to make a sudden descent. You all break formation with the *Flynut* and head further away, taking the hunters with you. When you're as far away as possible, turn off your lights to lose them and fly back to meet us at the castle.'

Francesca, who was leaning out of the front window to listen, took charge. 'Coco, Froggy,' she said urgently. 'Hang on! Shimmer, cut your light output.' The *Flynut* dramatically dropped out of formation. Coco and Froggy held on, their bodies dangling in mid-air.

'Okay, Shimmer,' said Francesca. 'Light on.'

Shimmer lit up brightly, muttering to herself. 'Light on, light off . . . make up your mind, Francesca.'

'Froggy, Coco, are you two okay out there?' shouted Francesca.

'Yes,' Coco replied. 'But hurry up and land, we can't hang on much longer!'

The *Flynut* came to a swift landing back at the castle, and Coco and Froggy climbed down, relieved to be safe.

'Francesca,' said Coco, 'help me drape the pirate flag over the *Flynut*, so that we can fly to Skye at first light.'

Eventually, the fireflies landed, telling Coco they had led the hunters many miles away from Nessie's eggs.

'Well done, guys,' said Coco. 'Go and have some well-earned honey.'

Chapter 10

Golden Eagle

As the *Flynut*, covered in the pirate flag, slowly flew out of the opening in the castle walls, Coco turned to Francesca and asked what the compass heading was.

'West,' said Francesca.

'Okay, Shimmer,' said Coco, 'increase light and move slightly forwards. We want to climb up to a thousand feet.'

'Open all hatches and windows,' ordered Francesca, 'and keep a lookout for crows!'

'I am absolutely famished,' said Shimmer. 'My light output is dimming!'

Coco told one of Shimmer's nieces to take her place. As soon as they swapped over, Coco realised that the *Flynut* was dramatically slowing down. The smaller firefly was putting out a lot less light than Shimmer. They were vulnerable to the crows!

Shimmer started to eat honey. As she looked out of the rear hatch of the mother craft, she noticed something.

'Coco, come over here. Look, in the distance. Can you make out those black specks following us?'

'Yes,' said Coco, 'it looks like Crook and her gang. Shimmer, get back on the skynut, NOW!'

'I can't,' replied Shimmer, 'I have to eat to get my energy levels back up.'

The crows began closing in, sensing that the *Flynut* was in trouble.

*　　*　　*

Francesca shouted, 'Isle of Skye, coming into view!'

'Good,' replied Coco. 'Tell me as soon as you see the Fairy Pools.' He turned back to his friend. 'Shimmer, are you ready yet?'

'No,' replied Shimmer, struggling to eat fast enough.

'The crows are almost on us!' cried Coco.

'Fairy Pools, up ahead!' said Francesca.

'Okay,' said Coco, 'change heading to north. Close all hatches and windows; the crows clearly aren't frightened of the pirate flag any more!'

The crows started to attack the *Flynut,* landing on top of it and pecking at it to knock it off course. Just when it was about to crash, a high-pitched screech from above scattered the attacking crows – apart from Hooper, who was grabbed by a huge pair of talons!

It was Hamish, the golden eagle.

As Hamish headed back to his nest with Hooper firmly gripped in his claws, back in the *Flynut* Coco told the crew to open all windows and hatches to find out what had happened.

Francesca spotted the eagle ahead of them. 'Quick, follow that giant bird,' she said.

'That must be Hamish,' said Coco, as the eagle landed on a ledge on the Old Man of Storr. 'We'll land at a safe distance away from him.'

As they all got out of the *Flynut*, Francesca shouted to Hamish, 'Don't eat that crow!'

Hamish turned to her and replied angrily, 'Who are you, telling me what to do? I'll eat you next.'

Hastily, Coco explained about their mission and that Nessie had guided them here.

'I can't help you. I'm getting old, and it took all my strength to catch this crow. But why do you care if I eat him? He was going to eat you.'

'He spared me and Coco on Comet Island,' Francesca replied.

Hamish ignored her, but Hooper said, 'You can't eat me! I'm on the endangered species list!'

'You look like a normal crow to me,' replied Hamish.

'Look at the hoop around my leg. I am a special crow,' pleaded Hooper.

Hamish released his grip on Hooper, knowing that the crow had been injured and couldn't fly now anyway. Hamish explained that Hooper should not be alive as his talons should have killed him, but Hamish wasn't as strong as he used to be. 'I can still kill him with my beak!'

'No, no,' said Coco. 'Hamish, would you fly back with us to Comet Island and rid our island of crows?

'I would if I could, but I don't have the strength. So I'll have to eat Hooper.'

The crow cowered away from Hamish. 'Pleeease don't!'

Francesca intervened. 'Hamish, if we strapped a skynut and a firefly to each of your wings it would give you extra power.'

'Okay,' said Hamish. 'But I'm hungry now.' He looked at Hooper again.

Coco came up with a solution. 'Froggy, can you bring out one of our emergency skynuts and give it to Hamish?'

When Froggy had done so, Hamish looked at the skynut uncertainly. 'What am I meant to do with this?' he asked.

'Eat it,' said Coco. 'It's full of energy and protein.'

Hamish swallowed the skynut in one gulp. 'That's even tastier than crow.' He smiled at Hooper.

Hooper smiled back and said, 'Coco, Francesca, thanks for saving my life. Can we be friends now? That includes you, Hamish.'

'That's a yes from me,' said Coco.

'And a yes from me,' said Francesca.

'And . . . and . . . yes from me,' said Hamish.

Everyone laughed and they all settled down for the night. For the first time no one was frightened, because they were all under Hamish's protection.

Chapter 11

Return to Comet Island

The sun came up, warming everyone on the small ledge on top of the Old Man of Storr. *We're finally heading back to save Comet Island*, Coco thought.

'Francesca, help me secure the skynuts to Hamish's wings,' he said.

'This is no good. They're not going to stay in place,' replied Francesca. 'But I have an idea. Why not use Hamish's nest feathers to weave the skynuts and fireflies into his wings?'

'Let's try it,' said Coco.

'That looks good and secure,' said Hamish, when they were done. 'Now, give my new little buddy Hooper a hand to get on my back, and use some of my larger feathers to weave him on.'

The creatures did what he said.

'Okay, crew, give me a hand to drape the pirate flag over the *Flynut*,' said Coco.

'That won't scare the crows. They've got used it,' replied Francesca.

'The ones on Comet Island haven't seen the flag yet,' insisted Coco.

At last all the preparations for the flight were complete. Coco spoke to his crew, Hamish with his fireflies, and Hooper.

'The *Flynut* will take off first then, Hamish, you will follow. We'll head south back to Comet Island, following the Gulf Stream.'

The *Flynut* hovered and moved away from the ledge, then descended to watch Hamish take off.

Hamish looked at his fireflies and instructed, 'Start your light output.'

They responded, and he began to stretch his enormous wings . . . Then, without flapping them, he slowly moved upwards.

'This is amazing. There's no pain. My

arthritis has gone,' said Hamish as he turned his head to look at Hooper.

Tilting his wings downwards, he instructed his fireflies to move forwards on their skynuts.

Hamish suddenly started to go into a dive!

Coco, who had been watching the take off, realised what was happening and put the *Flynut* into a dive as well, to catch up with Hamish. Coco matched the eagle's speed and shouted out of the window, 'I'm going to move in below you and give you extra lift!'

'Go for it,' replied Hamish.

The *Flynut* gently moved under Hamish.

'Okay, give me maximum power, Shimmer,' called Coco.

Slowly, Hamish was pushed up, narrowly missing a rock outcrop. 'That was close!' protested Hooper. 'What went wrong?'

'It was just a matter of Hamish and his fireflies learning to work together,' said Coco.

Hamish and the *Flynut* both levelled out at a higher altitude and headed south, with Hamish practising how to fly with his fireflies and skynuts.

*   *   *

Meanwhile, back on Comet Island, the animals in the dome were under attack by hungry crows who were trying to break in. Chester noticed that the roots were beginning to unravel and ordered all the bats inside to fly up to the ceiling and cling to the plug to stop the crows lifting it off!

Outside, the crows had formed a circle. They gripped the reeds around the plug and began to pull. Slowly, the plug started to move.

Chester called to everyone to evacuate the dome through the tunnel.

'No!' shouted Grandpa, as he ran down the tunnel. 'The crows are everywhere outside, on the ground and in the air!' As he looked up at the dome plug that was slowly beginning to lift, he shouted out in despair, 'Coco, where are you?'

*   *   *

As Coco, his crew, Hamish and Hooper

approached Comet Island they could see that the dome was under attack by hundreds of crows!

'Listen up,' said Coco, addressing his crew and Hamish. 'What we have to do is fly under Hamish's talons. When I give the word, we'll all dive down together, straight towards the dome, and scatter the crows. But before we do that, I want Batty and Froggy to separate their ships from *Mother*.'

'How do we do that?' asked Batty.

'Well,' said Coco, 'as we dive I want you and Froggy to reverse power on your ships and I'll increase power forwards in *Mother*. This will cause the magnets on all three ships to slide apart and separate. It'll really frighten the crows when we all break off and fly in different directions.'

Everyone nodded.

Coco shouted, 'Dive! Dive! Dive!'

Hamish tilted his wings forwards and let out an ear-piercing *screeeeeeech*! As they sped downwards, Hamish's wide wings cast a massive shadow over the dome. This made all the crows look skyward. When they saw what was speeding towards them, they immediately dropped the plug to the side of the dome and took flight.

Batty and Froggy instantly separated from *Mother*, going off in different directions. Hamish let out another screech as he got closer to the dome. This even frightened Hooper on his back. Coco went in the opposite direction to Hamish and as a result, the crows were totally confused and terrified, flying as far away as possible, to the outer edges of the island.

Coco, Batty and Froggy all landed inside the dome, where they were welcomed with an enormous cheer from all the animals inside.

Coco found his grandpa, who said, 'Coco, you saved us in the nick of time!'

'No,' said Coco. 'Hamish the eagle . . . he's the one we should all thank!'

A confused Grandpa looked up to the rim of the plughole where Hamish was perched. 'Why has he got a crow on his back?' he asked.

'It's a long story,' replied Coco, 'but first we

have to chase all the crows away from Comet Island!'

Chester called everyone together. 'First, let me say a big thank you to Coco and his team. I had my doubts, but Coco and his crew came through. Now that the crows are terrified, we have to make sure they leave our island!'

'Thank you, Chester,' said Coco. 'Time is of the essence. My plan to get rid of the crows involves Hamish and Hooper, plus myself and Francesca in *Mother*, Froggy in *Port* and Batty in *Star*. We will all fly to the south of the island and then position ourselves, widely spaced, along the coastline and start heading north, sweeping all the crows in front of us. When we have them all together over the sea to the north of the island, Hamish will approach the lead crow and fly alongside her. Hooper will then give the lead crow directions to fly to Scotland, where there is plenty of food and land for everyone.'

'Sounds like a good plan,' replied Chester. 'The only problem I see is when Hamish flies alongside the lead crow. Surely the lead crow will be frightened and try to escape!'

'I've thought of that. *Port* and *Star* will come up from below and box the lead crow in.'

'Okay,' Chester agreed. 'Make it happen.'

Coco and his friends flew to the south of the island and started the sweep north.

'Coco, a few crows are managing to escape from us!' said Hamish, flying alongside him.

'That's okay,' said Coco. 'We can live with a few of them on our island.'

Soon, the majority of crows were forced off the island, out to sea.

'Now,' called Coco, 'let's put the second part of our plan into action.'

'Okay,' said Hamish, as he flew up alongside the lead crow.

The lead crow got a fright and tried to escape, but was stopped from doing so by *Star* below him and *Port* to his left.

From Hamish's back, Hooper called to the lead crow . . . It was Crook!

Crook looked across at Hooper and snarled, 'You traitor!'

Hooper shouted back, 'You coward! You

were the first one to fly away from the golden eagle! Now, listen to me for once. Take all the crows back to Scotland, where there's plenty of food and land. You know the way.'

'Okay,' replied Crook, grudgingly, as she flew off into the distance.

Hamish, *Star* and *Port* descended and dropped back to meet up with *Mother* at the rear of the fleeing crows.

Coco and the rest of the team in *Mother* hovered to allow *Port* and *Star* to re-join with them. They all waved farewell to the fleeing crows, then headed back to the dome.

*   *   *

Grandpa and all the animals were waiting for the *Flynut*, Hamish and Hooper to return, standing outside the dome. As they landed, a huge cheer went up. Chester gave a speech praising all the flying heroes, particularly Coco for overcoming his shyness and saving Comet Island.

'Is there anything we can give you to show

our gratitude?' asked Chester.

Coco and Francesca were first. 'Can we keep the *Flynut*?'

'A big YES,' said Chester.

Froggy, Batty, Shimmer and her nephews and nieces were next. 'May we be the permanent crew of the *Flynut*?'

Chester thought for a moment then gave a big shout. 'Of course you can!'

Hamish was last. 'Can I stay on your island and make a nest on top of your dome?'

Chester was about to answer when Hamish went on, 'Oh, and can I take care of my little buddy Hooper?'

'Yes, yes, yes, yes, yes,' said Chester.

'And one more thing: can I have a lifetime supply of your delicious skynuts?'

Chester just nodded with a massive smile.

Everyone else smiled too, and looked at the sun setting on the blue horizon. Coco turned to Francesca and said, 'Let's get organised for our next mission: it's time to find Ben!'

Chapter 12

Phoenix Island

'I know you're all tired but I can't wait any longer,' said Coco to his team. 'Today we fly to Phoenix Island to rescue my friend Ben.'

'Okay,' agreed Francesca. 'What do you want us to do?'

'Well, we won't need so many supplies this time, as Phoenix Island is much closer than Scotland. That means you can come with us Dug, along with your digging skills.'

'I won't let you down,' said the delighted mole.

'It will be great having you on board,' said Coco. He turned to Hamish and asked, 'Could I borrow some of your nest feathers?'

'What for?' asked Hamish.

'We need to land in the clearing that belongs to the humans on the island. I asked Hooper and Chip to join us on the mission, and they told me I'll have to disguise the *Flynut* as a bird to do that,' replied Coco.

'The clearing is totally surrounded by rabbit holes with rabbits feeding, giving the impression all is well,' explained Chip. 'The humans scatter food to lure us birds and . . . catch us!'

'So, we have a plan – and the plan is not to get caught,' said Coco. 'First, Hooper, are you well enough to fly?'

'Yes,' said Hooper, eager to be in the air again.

'Good,' said Coco. 'You, Hamish and Chip, will land in the clearing first, to divert attention away from the *Flynut*. The *Flynut* will descend into the widest rabbit hole we can see, then you three will quickly make your escape.' He paused, then continued, 'Okay, everyone aboard the *Flynut*. Hooper, you and Chip take the lead. We will hide below

Hamish to escape detection. Shimmer, start your light, full power.'

The *Flynut* took off from outside the Old Hollow Tree. Coco had no need to worry about crows attacking them now.

'Looks like we're flying south,' said Francesca, as she watched Hooper and Chip leading the way.

'This is simply fantastic!' said Dug to Coco.

'It sure is,' replied Coco. 'It must beat digging underground. But we might need your skills in the rabbit tunnels.'

'No problem,' replied Dug.

'Phoenix Island coming up straight ahead,' said Francesca excitedly. 'Hooper and Chip have started their descent.'

'Okay, Shimmer, move slightly forwards and reduce your light output gradually,' said Coco.

'Hamish is flying above us and following our movements,' said Francesca.

Froggy looked across at Batty and said, 'Here we go again!'

'There's a clearing up ahead,' said Francesca. 'Look at all those rabbit holes around the sides. Which one, Coco?'

'I can't see any hole wide enough for the *Flynut*! Okay, we'll have to split up. Remember that manoeuvre we did when we dived at the crows on the dome and separated the coconuts?'

'Yes,' replied Batty and Froggy.

'When I give the word, separate from *Mother*, then fly into the rabbit hole nearest to you and start searching for Ben.'

'Hamish is about to land with Hooper and Chip,' said Francesca.

'Okay, start separation of the ships . . . But first, six fireflies go into *Port* and six into *Star*,' shouted Coco.

As Hamish flared his wings to land, Hooper and Chip swept to either side of him to distract any humans who might be watching. The *Flynut* split up and each ship headed into its nearest rabbit hole.

'Open the rear hatch,' Coco shouted anxiously. 'Let's see if Hamish and his team have escaped!'

Francesca raced to the back of *Mother* to

look out of the hatch. 'They've been captured by the humans!' she said. 'And there's a human hand reaching in here! It's trying to grab us with its fingertips!'

Coco froze with fear for a moment, then came to his senses.

'Quick, Shimmer, move forwards – max light,' he shouted.

'But we can't see what's in front of us!' protested Francesca.

'Just do it. Anything to get us out of the human's reach,' said Coco.

They surged forwards. 'We've made it just far enough away from the hand,' Francesca reported.

'Okay, close the hatch,' said Coco. 'We don't want the human to see our light. Now, let's take stock of the situation. Hamish, Hooper and Chip have been captured, and will probably be taken to the bird sanctuary where Hooper and Chip were taken before. Froggy and Batty are in different tunnels and we can't see where we're going!'

'It does look grim,' said Francesca. 'What

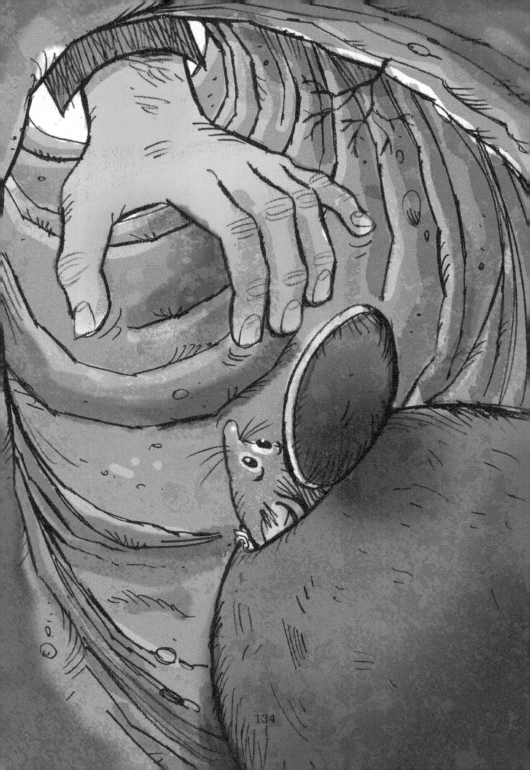

are we going to do?'

Coco thought for a moment. 'First,' he said, 'Shimmer, can you ask one of your nieces or nephews to put their light through the front lower window to light up the way ahead?'

'Yes,' said Shimmer.

'This is amazing!' said Dug as *Mother* started moving. 'Look at the number of tunnels going off in different directions. These rabbits know how to dig . . .' He trailed off, then burst out, 'Stop! Turn left! Froggy just shot past us!'

'Okay,' said Coco, 'follow that coconut!'

*   *   *

Looking out through *Port*'s rear hatch, Froggy said to Day, 'Lower your beam. There's a light coming towards us.'

'Go dark, Shimmer,' said Coco, as *Mother* bumped into *Port*.

'Hello,' said Froggy as he popped his head through *Mother*'s front window.

'Good to see you, Froggy,' replied Coco. 'There's no room for us to rotate. I want you to reverse against *Mother*, and we'll also reverse back to the open area where Dug spotted you.'

'Understood,' replied Froggy as they reversed back to the open area and landed.

As Coco got out of *Mother*, a young rabbit approached him.

'Hello,' said Coco. 'I guess you're a rabbit?' he asked, thinking of the description Chip had given him.

'Yes, I am. My name is Lucky. What's yours?'

'My name is Coco, and we're here searching for my friend Ben.'

'Oh, Ben. He mentioned you,' said Lucky.

Coco's face lit up. 'That's brilliant. Can you take me to him?'

'I'm afraid not. He disappeared down the forbidden tunnel,' said Lucky.

'Why did he do that?' asked Coco.

'He was desperate to go home, so he dug a small hole into the forbidden tunnel that we had filled back up,' said Lucky.

'Why would he do that?' asked Coco.

'Legend has it that the tunnel leads to freedom, away from humans,' replied Lucky.

Just then, Batty gently landed *Star* next to them. 'Hello,' he said. 'Thank goodness we've found you all.'

'Hold on a minute, Batty,' said Coco. 'Lucky, why did your rabbits block the forbidden tunnel? Don't they want freedom?'

'Because the rabbits that went down there never came back to tell us if it was safe,' said Lucky. Coco began to think he might be too late to save Ben and went quiet.

'Come on, Coco,' said Francesca. 'Don't give up.'

'Okay,' said Coco, snapping out of his sadness. 'Lucky, can you show Dug the way to the forbidden tunnel?'

'Yes,' said Lucky, bounding away. 'Dug, follow me.'

It didn't take long to reach the tunnel. 'Okay, Dug, start to dig,' said Coco. 'Make it big enough to get *Mother* through.'

'Hold on,' said Batty, 'is that a good idea?'

'Yes,' replied Coco, 'because if we go back the way we came in, we'll probably be captured by the humans. Plus I've got to find Ben!

While Dug is digging, I want *Star* and *Port* to line up behind *Mother*.'

'Why do we have to do that?' asked Francesca.

'Well, we don't know what's down there,' replied Coco. 'This formation will help us stay together and give us maximum protection.'

'Everyone, help move away all the earth Dug has been digging out,' instructed Francesca.

'We're almost finished,' called Dug, working in the light of his two fireflies.

'Dug, let me past you,' said Coco, scraping a small hole in the dirt to look through.

'What can you see, Coco?' asked Francesca, anxiously.

'It's too dark to be sure, but it looks like a large cavern, with a small shaft of light in the distance.' Coco thought for a moment and added, 'It's not safe to allow Dug to finish digging the tunnel. We don't know what's behind the remaining soil. This is what we're going to do. When I give the word, all three ships will move forwards together, pushing what's left of the earth into the cavern. Okay.

Froggy, Batty, full power! Start moving forwards!'

After a moment, Francesca said, 'We're through.'

'Okay, maintain hover. All fireflies scatter throughout the cavern. Everyone start looking for Ben!' said Coco.

'This is a strange place,' said Batty. 'What's all this white sticky stuff?'

Suddenly, Coco shouted out, 'Over there, in that corner, covered in the white stuff! Is it Ben?'

Francesca shrieked. 'There, on the wall . . . It's a huge, black, hairy TARANTULA! And it's heading towards Ben!'

'Not if I can help it!' said Coco. 'Shimmer, let's fly down to take a closer look.'

As *Mother* hovered near the white-covered shape, Coco shouted, 'It *is* Ben!'

The tarantula scurried between *Mother* and Ben, lifted its front legs in the air and exposed two large, glistening fangs. It was ready to attack!

'I have an idea. Quickly, Shimmer, turn

your tail towards it and flash as brightly as you can,' Coco instructed, hoping his plan would work.

Just as the tarantula was about to pounce, Shimmer let out a brilliant burst of light. The spider stopped instantly, stunned by the intense brightness.

'Quickly, Francesca!' urged Coco. 'Ben's dazed, but he's still alive. Help me get him into *Mother*.'

'He's too heavy,' screamed Francesca as they tried, 'and the tarantula's starting to move!'

'Just push . . .' cried Coco. 'That's it, he's in! Shimmer, get back on the skynut, full power!'

The *Mother* ship slowly started to lift as the tarantula came to its senses and jumped after them, just missing the open side of the craft with its hook-like fangs.

'Okay, rejoin the formation in front of *Port* and *Star* and head for the distant light. That must be the way out,' said Coco.

As the three ships headed for the exit light, Francesca cried out, 'Look up ahead, there are three tarantulas waiting for us at the exit!'

'All three ships, full power!' commanded Coco.

'You got it!' said Shimmer, just as she began to slip off of the skynut.

'The three tarantulas are forming a net across the exit with their legs!' shouted Francesca.

'Francesca, quickly, help me put Shimmer back on the skynut,' said Coco. 'Just one more push, Francesca . . . Okay, full power, Shimmer.'

The *Flynut* accelerated to top speed. It smashed its way through the three tarantulas and out into the bright blue sky.

'Francesca, tell Froggy and Batty to come alongside *Mother* and reattach,' ordered Coco as he tore away the spidery web encasing Ben with his paws.

'Thank you! Thank you, Coco!' cried a terrified Ben. 'I knew you'd come to rescue me.'

'I'm sorry it took so long,' replied Coco as he hugged his best friend.

'*Port* and *Star* are rejoining us,' said Francesca, interrupting their hug.

'Good,' said Coco. 'Now, let's find the aviary where Hamish, Hooper and Chip are imprisoned.'

'Coco, you've changed,' said a grateful Ben. 'You're so brave.'

'Well, I had to be to find you,' replied Coco, overcome with emotion.

'Coco, Coco!' exclaimed Francesca. 'Batty and Froggy say one of the tarantulas is hanging on to the underside of *Mother*!'

'I thought we were climbing slowly when we escaped the rabbit hole! The tarantula must have been weighing us down. But we're safe inside the *Flynut*,' replied Coco.

'We're over the aviary,' shouted Batty, 'and I can see Hamish.'

'Shimmer, start your descent and hover just outside the gate,' said Coco.

'Look, Coco,' said Froggy. 'That human is opening the gate. He's got food.'

'It's our chance to solve two problems!' said Coco. 'We need to get rid of the spider *and* keep an escape route open. We've got to time this to the second, Shimmer. Now, move towards the human's shoulder, up a bit . . . too much, drop slightly, and hold that position . . . Just as he opens the gate, we want to brush his shoulder,dropping the tarantula onto it.'

As the human opened the gate, he turned his head to see what was happening behind him. To his amazement, heading straight towards him were three coconuts, with a tarantula hanging below them . . . He didn't duck fast enough and the next moment, there on his right shoulder was a big, black, hairy tarantula, and it was crawling towards his head!

'Bingo! Well done, Coco, the human is panicking and has left the gate wide open,' said Francesca, looking out of the rear hatch.

'Now it's up to Hamish, Hooper and Chip to seize their chance to escape,' said Coco.

* * *

Down in the aviary, Hamish saw what had happened and realised he had to move fast. 'Come on, guys, give me max light,' he said to his fireflies. 'That's it. Hooper, get Chip and follow me.'

'Hamish, you'll have to pull in your wings to get through the gate!' said Hooper.

'Yes, I will,' replied Hamish. He rose into the air to get some speed and then pulled in his wings and held them close to his body as he dived through the gate. As he opened his wings he knocked the tarantula off of the man's shoulder.

'Good to have you all back,' Coco shouted across to Hamish, Hooper and Chip as they flew alongside the *Flynut.* 'Why did you help the human, Hamish?'

'I hate seeing an animal in distress,' Hamish replied.

'Okay, let's all head for home,' said Coco.

*   *   *

As the *Flynut* arrived back over Comet Island, all the animals rushed out of the Old Hollow Tree, cheering their return. Ben's mum was at the front of the crowd, holding her breath.

Slowly, the *Flynut* started its descent and landed gently, with Hamish, Hooper and Chip alongside.

The crowd went silent as the crew came out one by one, none of them smiling. Then Ben popped his head out from around the hatch, smiling from ear to ear, and said, 'Hi, Mum!'

'Oh, Ben! My boy is back home,' shouted his mum, overjoyed as she hugged him. 'Thank you all – but especially THANK YOU, Coco!'

Coco glowed with pride as he smiled back at Ben's mum. He had rescued Ben with the help of his new friends, who had supported

him on their adventures and motivated him to overcome his shyness. He was now a confident mouse!

Then he turned to address the crowd. 'There's something else,' he said. 'During our search in Scotland, two children called Corey and Freya helped us find our friend Hamish, but they also told us that Comet Island could be in danger again because of a thing called climate change.'

The crowd gasped.

'But I have an idea that can help the humans stop climate change . . . skynuts! Let's make plans for our return mission to Scotland!'

The End

JAMES HALLIDAY STAGE was born in 1952 in Aberdeen, Scotland to an English mother and a Scottish father. After leaving school he went to college and completed an apprenticeship as an electrician. He has been an inventor and designer. He loves aviation and space, and has flown solo Cessna 150 and microlight aircraft and hang-gliders. He still enjoys riding his motorbike and is currently rebuilding an Isetta 300 bubble car. When his three sons Mark, Richard, and Scott, were children he would make up his own ad-libbed bedtime stories for them. *Saving Comet Island* is his first book.